Interest Level: Gr 4-8
AR pts: 1.0
ATOS Book Level: 3.1

TJ TRAPPER BULLY ZAPPER

TJ Zaps a Nightmare
Stopping Blackmail Bullying

magic Wagon

BOOK
5

written by
Lisa Mullarkey

illustrated by
Gary LaCoste

visit us at www.abdopublishing.com

To the brave kid who rang the doorbell to say he was sorry — LM
For Ashley — GL

Published by Magic Wagon, a division of the ABDO Group,
PO Box 398166, Minneapolis, MN 55439. Copyright © 2013 by
Abdo Consulting Group, Inc. International copyrights reserved
in all countries. All rights reserved. No part of this book may
be reproduced in any form without written permission from the
publisher.

Calico Chapter Books™ is a trademark and logo of Magic Wagon.

Printed in the United States of America, North Mankato, Minnesota.
052012
092012
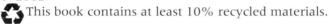 This book contains at least 10% recycled materials.

Text by Lisa Mullarkey
Illustrations by Gary LaCoste
Edited by Stephanie Hedlund and Rochelle Baltzer
Cover and interior design by Neil Klinepier

Library of Congress Cataloging-in-Publication Data
Mullarkey, Lisa.
  TJ zaps a nightmare : stopping blackmail bullying / by Lisa
Mullarkey ; illustrated by Gary LaCoste.
      p. cm. -- (TJ Trapper, bully zapper ; bk. 5)
  Summary: When TJ cheats on a history test and gets chosen to
represent his school in a contest, he feels horribly guilty--worse, he
finds himself being blackmailed for money by one of his classmates.
  ISBN 978-1-61641-909-7
  1. Bullying--Juvenile fiction. 2. Extortion--Juvenile fiction. 3.
Cheating (Education)--Juvenile fiction. 4. Schools--Juvenile fiction.
5. Friendship--Juvenile fiction. [1. Bullies--Fiction. 2. Extortion-
-Fiction. 3. Cheating--Fiction. 4. Schools--Fiction. 5. Friendship--
Fiction.] I. LaCoste, Gary, ill. II. Title.
  PZ7.M91148Tjo 2012
  813.6--dc23
                                              2012008067

Contents

Tea Party Time?

On Monday morning, I couldn't wait to go to school. By Monday afternoon, I never wanted to go back.

When I got there, I wanted to play basketball before the bell rang. But my friends were sitting on the ground with their noses in notebooks.

"What's up?" I asked as I spun the ball on my finger. "Aren't we shootin' hoops?"

Livvy sighed. "Salutations, TJ. We're studying for the test."

"Test?" I asked. "What test?"

"Shhh," Lamar hissed as he chewed on his nail. "I need to concentrate."

"You studied, didn't you?" asked Maxi. "You always study."

"Not exactly," I said. "I sort of forgot about it."

Livvy's eyes bugged out. "Sort of forgot? How can you *sort of* forget?"

I shrugged as I looked over her shoulder. "The Boston Tea Party? I got a 100 on the quiz last week. I'll pass it."

"Ms. Perry said it's a tough test," said Livvy. "You'll fail it if you didn't study."

I twirled the basketball on my finger again. "I have all hundreds in social studies. I'm not going to fail it." Then I added, "I hope."

Everyone's noses dipped back into their notebooks. "Come on, guys," I said. "Who wants to shoot some hoops?"

Maxi snapped her notebook shut. "I will. I need a break. I'm starting to mix up the dates."

"Dates?" I asked. "Do we need to know *exact* dates?"

Maxi nodded and grabbed the basketball from my hands. "What year did the Boston Tea Party take place?"

"December 16, 1773," I said without thinking.

Maxi nodded. "You'll ace it." Then *she* added, "I hope."

So while Maxi and I shot free throws, everyone else studied.

"We'll practice at recess," Ethan yelled as I sunk my first one.

But Ethan ended up going to the library to study at recess. So did Livvy, Maxi, Lamar, Kyle, and Kelli.

"Want to come with us?" asked Livvy. "Ms. Perry warned us that it's going to be the hardest test in the world."

Maxi laughed. "She didn't say in the world. Just the hardest one she's given."

"I studied a little during free reading," I said. Then I looked out the window at the fifth graders playing basketball. "I'm going to play ball."

After lunch, Livvy begged Ms. Perry to let her study more. Ms. Perry frowned. "If you don't know it by now, Livvy, it's too late." She patted Livvy on the back. "Besides, you've studied all day. I'm sure you'll do fine. As long as you've looked over the study guide . . . "

"Study guide?" I whispered. Before I had a chance to whip it out, Ms. Perry plopped a test on my desk.

I glanced down at the first page and wrote my name and the date. That was the easy part! Then I answered three short essays. No problem! If you listened to Ms. Perry talk in class, you'd be able to ace all of them.

Then I got to page two.

Each multiple choice question is worth 2 points.

I scanned the thirty questions. My hands started to sweat.

I only knew half of them. Half.

How much was the tea worth?

I had no clue.

How many pounds of tea were dumped overboard?

Pounds? No idea.

How many people dressed up as Native Americans and took part in the dumping?

Was it 216? 125? 116? 300?

I was going to have to guess. On half of them! Thirty points worth of guessing!

No one else seemed to be guessing. Ethan was flying through the columns of questions. Every time he knew an answer, he'd nod his head and pump his fist. To the left, Livvy did the same.

As I glanced at my basketball on the shelf, I got a sinking feeling. This would be the first test I'd ever failed.

That's when Livvy suddenly leaned way to the right. Her test teetered on the edge of her desk. Her handwriting was really big. So big that I could easily see all her answers. So big that I bet people living in Boston could see her answers! Then quicker than the Indians threw the tea into the harbor, I copied down all of them.

B-C-A-A-A-A-D-D-D-A-A-B-B-A-C.

Before I copied the second column, I waited until Ms. Perry bent over to talk to

Lamar. Once I was sure no one was looking, I copied the rest of Livvy's answers.

D-C-C-B-A-A-A-C-D-B-A-B-A-C-A.

Just as I finished writing the last one, Ms. Perry announced, "Time's up. Pass your papers forward."

"How did you do?" Livvy asked as she passed her test forward.

"I think I got an A," I said as I stuffed my hands in my pocket. "Maybe an A minus."

"You don't look too happy about it," said Maxi. "Smile!" She made a funny face before she turned serious. "I wish I was as smart as you, TJ."

My face burned. I didn't feel so smart.

Nope, I felt like a loser. An A+ cheater.

The Challenge

When Ms. Perry handed back the tests after art, I wanted to crawl under my desk.

"TJ," said Ms. Perry, "you got another 100." She hung my test on the bulletin board. "I'm not surprised." Then she added, "I'm so proud of you for always studying so hard."

"Ha!" came a whisper from behind me. I whipped my neck around to see who it was. Was it Lamar? Kyle? I couldn't tell.

I glanced over at the board. Livvy's paper was below mine. It should have been above mine.

"Congratulations, Livvy," I said. "You got an A, too."

She sighed. "But it wasn't a 100 like yours. It was only a 93." She stomped her foot. "That first essay was so hard!" She put the back of her hand on her forehead. "My average is gone forever. Forever and ever!"

"You still got an A," I said. "A 93 is a great grade."

Livvy stuck her nose in the air. "That's easy for you to say, TJ. You *got* a perfect score."

If she only knew . . .

Ethan tossed his test on his desk. It had a big 71 at the top of it. "You said you didn't study, TJ," Ethan said. "How did you get a 100?"

Lamar walked over. "That's what I want to know. You must have studied or you would have failed." He glanced at Ethan's test. "Or have gotten a 71."

Ethan stuck his tongue out at Lamar.

I shrugged and walked away. I didn't want to talk about my grade. All I wanted to do was rip my paper off of the bulletin board and throw it in the trash. That's where it belonged. Every time I thought about cheating off of Livvy, I felt like someone kicked me in the stomach.

Five minutes later, Ms. Perry made an announcement. "Class," she said, "I have exciting news. Our school is participating in the Red, White, and Blue Social Studies Challenge. It's sort of like a spelling bee.

Does everyone remember how a spelling bee works? We just had one in class."

Twenty-three heads bobbed up and down.

"In this competition, kids are asked questions about American history," said Ms. Perry. "Fourth graders will be tested on the American Revolution."

She slowly rubbed her hands together and raised her eyebrows as she glanced at me. "It's what we've been studying the past few months."

I tried to smile at her, but I couldn't.

"One student from grades four, five, and six will each get to participate in the Challenge," she said. "If you win the local round, you'll compete at the state level. If you win that, you'll travel with your family to compete in Washington DC!"

Everyone cheered as hands flew into the air.

"Can I go?" shouted Ethan.

"I want to go," said Lamar as he waved his hand wildly.

"Me too," said Kelli. "It would be so much fun!"

Ms. Perry opened her grade book. "It will be an exciting and fun competition. But only one student from our class can participate. To be fair, I've looked over all of your grades and took tests, quizzes, and projects into consideration." She snapped the book shut. "And based on that data, I've decided who'll represent our class."

Hands flew back into the air as kids jumped out of their chairs. Besides me, Livvy was the only kid who wasn't waving her hand. Instead, her hands were folded in front of her chest. Her chin was on top of them and her eyes were shut tight. She rocked slowly back and forth.

Ms. Perry cleared her throat. "The student who will represent us in the Red, White, and Blue Challenge is . . ."

Ethan and Lamar pounded their hands on their desks for a drumroll.

"TJ Trapper," said Ms. Perry as she rushed forward and hugged me. "I know you'll make us proud, TJ."

I felt like I had been double karate chopped. Ethan gave me a high five.

"Congrats! You're so lucky! Washington DC!" Ethan exclaimed.

"It's not luck," said Kelli. "He studies all the time."

Maxi jumped up and down. "Maybe you'll meet the president!"

Livvy opened her eyes and held out her hand. "Congratulations, TJ. You deserve to go."

If she only knew . . .

As I shook her hand, I noticed her lip quivering. She was about to cry.

Now I was about to lose it. I knew that there was no way I deserved it. I felt guilty. I tried to push the feeling away by promising myself that I would never cheat again. Ever. It wasn't worth it.

But after Ms. Perry showed me the challenge Web site and pictures of the winners with the president, I stopped thinking about cheating and started to get excited.

I mean, if I had studied like I usually did, I would have aced it. Right? Ten minutes later, I was starting to feel pretty good about things until I walked into the coatroom to pack up. That's when I noticed a note sitting on the top of my locker.

To TJ Cheater

From Your Worst Nightmare

Was this a joke? My heart raced as I opened it. Then it sunk when I read the five words inside:

I SAW WHAT YOU DID.

Nightmare Calls

I jumped off the bus, ran straight inside my house, and bolted up the stairs to my room. I unfolded the note and read it again.

To TJ Cheater

From Your Worst Nightmare

I SAW WHAT YOU DID.

I lifted my mattress and stashed the note underneath. Just then, Auntie Stella knocked on my door.

"What's the rush, mister? No kiss for Auntie Stella?" She leaned over and pecked me on the cheek.

"Sorry," I said. "I had to go to the bathroom."

She squinted her eyes. "What's wrong with the bathroom downstairs?"

Auntie Stella could smell a lie a mile away. Then she stared at my bed. "Stop fussing with that bed. I changed your sheets today. Made it up nice and fresh. The mattress looks crooked."

I jammed my knee into the side of it and pushed it back into place. "Sorry."

She smiled and swung her hand around in the air. "You don't want me to have to give you the old dish towel, do you?"

If she knew I was a cheater, I'd get more than the old dish towel.

She grabbed my hands and pulled me toward the door. "Come have some Crispy Treats. They're still warm."

"No thanks, Auntie Stella."

She felt my forehead. "Not hungry for Crispy Treats? Something must be wrong."

"Nothing's wrong," I said as I walked by her and headed down the stairs.

When we got to the kitchen, the phone rang.

"Let it ring," she said. "All day long, that phone rings. Someone is always trying to sell me something. Do I look like I need new windows? A cleaning service? Diapers?"

"It could be Ethan," I said as I grabbed the phone.

But it wasn't Ethan.

"Is this TJ *Cheater*?" asked a girl's voice.

I sucked in my breath and turned away from Auntie Stella.

My voice shook. "Yes."

"I saw what you did," said the voice. "You cheated. If you don't want me to tell, leave a candy bar and a dollar in a brown bag right where you found the note."

Click.

I hung up the phone and bit my lip. *Whose voice was that?*

"You look like you've seen a ghost," said Auntie Stella. "Who was that?"

"My worst nightmare," I whispered.

"Speak up, TJ," said Auntie Stella. "My ears are old and tired."

"Just Ethan," I said. "We're going to play basketball in a little bit."

"Exercise is good for you!" said Auntie Stella as she handed me a glass of milk. "Drink up."

As I gulped it down, I stared at the cabinet above the stove. That's where Auntie Stella keeps a not-so-secret stash of junk food. "Auntie Stella, do you have any candy I can bring with me?"

"Eating junk food while exercising? That seems silly," she said. "Besides," she said in a loud voice, "I would never give you a candy bar before dinner." Then she looked out the back window and whispered. "I have a new Choco Caramel Crunch Bar that has your name on it. But if your father sees you eating it, I'll deny ever giving it to you. Got it?"

"Got it," I said.

She looked one last time out the window to make sure Dad wasn't home yet. "It will be our little secret," she said as she pushed the step stool toward the cabinet. A second later, she tossed two bars down to me. "One for you and one for Ethan."

I shoved them in my pocket. I sure hoped my worst nightmare liked Choco Caramel Crunch Bars. Whoever it was.

I stared at my class picture hanging on the fridge and ran my finger under each girl's face. The voice didn't sound like any of them. Who could it be?

While I was still thinking, the doorbell rang.

"It's Ethan," said Auntie Stella as she looked outside. She scratched her head. "Didn't he just call?"

"He used his cell phone," I said as I planted a kiss on her cheek. I grabbed my basketball. "I'll be home in an hour."

But Ethan had other plans.

As I tried to walk out the door, Ethan tried to walk in it. "So is Auntie Stella excited?"

"Excited about what?" said Auntie Stella. Her eyes lit up. "What's going on?"

Ethan rolled his eyes and pushed past me. "You didn't tell her yet? What are you waiting for?"

I stammered. "I . . . I . . ."

Ethan patted me on the back. "He might go to Washington DC to meet the president."

"Meet the president?" asked Dad as he closed the back door behind him. "Who's meeting the president?"

Auntie Stella clapped her hands. "TJ!"

I threw my hands up in the air. "No. Not me. Wait. I don't think I'm entering." I slid into a chair and rubbed my eyes.

Dad pulled out a chair and sat. "What's up, buddy?"

Before I had a chance to tell them, Ethan blurted it out.

"Ms. Perry said he's entering the Red, White, and Blue Challenge. It's like a spelling bee except this is for social studies. Since TJ has the best grades in social studies in our class, she picked him to compete in the challenge. If he beats the other fourth graders in the area, he goes to the state competition. If he wins that, he moves on to the national competition."

"It's in Washington DC," I said. "Last year everyone got to meet the president."

Dad and Auntie Stella high-fived each other. Then Dad grabbed Auntie Stella and started swinging her around the room. "This is called the My Son Is So Smart He's Going to Washington DC Dance!" yelled Dad as he twirled her around.

Auntie Stella huffed and puffed when she stopped twirling. "Just think, TJ. Maybe this is the beginning. First, you'll *meet* the president and then one day you'll *be* president."

Ethan laughed. "Yep. Just like President Obama, President Washington, President Roosevelt . . . "

"Don't forget Honest Abe," shouted Dad.

Great, I thought. *I'll go down in history as DIShonest TJ.*

Accusing Maxi

When I got to school the next day, I hurried into the coatroom. After making sure no one saw me, I pulled the brown bag out of my backpack. I peeked inside one last time to make sure the dollar was there, too. I tossed it on top of my locker. Now I had to watch the coatroom all day to see who took it.

When I got back to my desk, Ms. Perry was waiting. "Is your dad excited for you? I know Auntie Stella is thrilled.

She e-mailed me. She's so confident that you'll win the state level, that she's already packing for your trip to Washington."

I sucked in my breath. "Don't you think Livvy is smarter than me? I think she deserves to go more than I do."

Ms. Perry cocked her head to the side. "Why would you say that? You're very deserving. Your grades . . ."

"But Livvy has all As, too," I said.

"You have all 100s. I went with the highest grade average," said Ms. Perry. "I think you have a case of the jitters."

More like a case of the guilts, I thought.

Just then, I saw Kyle walk into the coatroom. After he came out, I rushed back inside to see if the bag was gone. It was still there. Then bus three arrived and the kids swarmed into the coatroom all at

once. I wanted to hang out by the door but Ms. Perry had other plans.

"TJ, could you please bring this note to the office for me?"

Just then, Lamar and Maxi headed toward the coatroom, too.

"Not right now, Ms. Perry," I said. "I have to do something."

Ms. Perry folded her arms across her chest. "You're already unpacked, TJ. And you're right. You *do* have to do something. Like take this to the office."

I smiled. "Um . . . sure. Sorry." So while I was going to the office, someone else was taking my candy bar and money. When I got back, the bag was gone! Kids from buses four, seven, and eight were unpacking their backpacks. It could have been anyone! It was going to be a lot harder to catch my worst nightmare than I thought it would be.

Or at least I thought so until lunchtime rolled around.

When I was cleaning up my lunch and throwing away my trash, I saw Maxi at her table eating a candy bar. But it wasn't just any candy bar. It was a Choco Caramel Crunch Bar!

Maxi was my worst nightmare!

I marched over to her. "So, it's you! Why didn't you just tell me instead of making me bring you candy? I know I did something stupid, but to call me and leave me such a mean note! I thought we were friends."

Maxi bit off a chunk of the bar. "What are you talking about?"

My eyes darted around the table to make sure no one was listening. "You know what I'm talking about."

She looked at me like I had a hundred heads. "No, I honestly have no idea."

I swiped the candy bar from her hand. "Then where did you get this?"

"From the vending machine at my mom's work yesterday," she said. She grabbed it back and took another bite. "If you don't believe me, you can ask her." Then she looked at my lunch box. "Why? Did someone take yours?"

My eyes got all watery.

"Don't cry, TJ. You can have the rest of mine," said Maxi.

I wiped my eyes. "I'm not crying. It's just that . . . just that . . ." I looked around the room. There were too many people nearby. "Can you meet me by the trash can when we go outside? I need your help."

She nodded.

Five minutes later, we were ducking behind a smelly garbage can.

"Before I show you something," I said, "do you swear to keep it a secret?"

Maxi crossed her heart with her finger. "Promise."

"I did something really stupid," I said.

Maxi didn't say anything.

"And then I got this," I said as I took the note from my pocket and handed it to her.

She read it and then gasped. "What did you do?" Then she covered her mouth. "You don't have to tell me if you don't want to. But maybe I can help." She reread the note again. "So what does the candy bar have to do with this?"

So I explained the phone call. The girl's voice. The candy and dollar bill that I left in the bag. "And now I'm afraid she's still going to tell even though I gave her what she wanted."

Maxi put her arm around my shoulder. "TJ, you're being blackmailed. I saw something just like this on TV. Whoever wrote this is probably going to keep telling you that you'll have to give her things . . . or else."

"Blackmail?" I said. "Blackmailing me for candy doesn't make sense."

"Yes, it does," said Maxi. "If you are afraid of getting in trouble, the person can blackmail you for anything she wants."

"Well, at least she only asked for a candy bar and a dollar," I said.

"This time," said Maxi. Then she bit her lip. "Did you cheat on the test? Is that how you got the 100?"

I nodded. "I feel awful about it. Livvy should be entering the competition. What should I do?"

Maxi held up her hands in the air. "Don't ask me." Then she added, "Maybe you should tell Ms. Perry."

"No way," I said. "I'll get in so much trouble. My dad and Auntie Stella will be mad. I'll be grounded."

Maxi sighed. "I'm not going to tell anyone. But I think you should. Blackmailing someone is way worse than what you did, TJ."

I sighed. "At least that part's over."

But it wasn't over. When recess ended, I found a piece of paper folded in half on my chair.

Unless you leave me five dollars in a brown bag tomorrow, everyone will know your secret. EVERYONE.

I ripped the paper to shreds as fast as I could. Great. Where was I going to get five dollars?

Snapped!

When I got home, Auntie Stella had hung up a sign in the kitchen.

Congratulations, TJ!

"I haven't won anything yet," I reminded her. I peeled the tape off the sign and started to take it down.

"But you will," said Auntie Stella as she taped it back into place. "You will." She took off her apron and opened the oven. The smell of onions and garlic rushed out.

My mouth watered. "Did you make lasagna?"

"Of course! It's a celebration dinner! Your father and I are so proud of you. I'm going to make all of your favorite foods until the local round is over."

I suddenly lost my appetite.

Auntie Stella started to ask me a million questions about the American Revolution. I missed a few.

"Eight out of ten right is very good, TJ," said Auntie Stella. "Good enough to win, I think."

I took my folder out of my backpack and muttered, "Livvy would have known all of them."

"Then ask Livvy to help you study," said Auntie Stella.

"No way!" I shouted. "I could never ask her. It wouldn't be right."

Auntie Stella gave me an odd look. "It wouldn't be wrong either, now would it?"

I shrugged and started my homework. That's when the phone rang. I jumped up to grab it.

But Auntie Stella beat me to it.

"Hello?" Then she cleared her throat and repeated it. "Hello?" She twitched her nose and raised her eyebrows. "No one's there." She hung up.

I had a funny feeling that I knew who it was: my worst nightmare.

And I was right. Fifteen minutes later, while Auntie Stella was downstairs doing laundry, the phone rang again.

"Don't forget the five dollars tomorrow or else . . ." said the voice on the other end.

"Or else what?" I whispered into the receiver.

"Or else everyone will know you're a fake. And a cheater."

Click.

And a loser, I thought.

After dinner was over, Dad came up to my room. "Hey buddy, isn't there something you've been meaning to tell me?"

"Like what?" I stammered.

"Like you need this," he said as he tossed a five-dollar bill onto my bed.

"How did you know?" I said. "I wanted to tell you but . . ."

"It's okay," said Dad. "I'm just glad I remembered the due date since you clearly forgot."

I must have looked confused because Dad held up my book order. "You wanted to buy the next book in that series we were reading, didn't you? It's due tomorrow. Fair is fair. You finished the first one before I did. You win a book."

I faked a smile. "Oh, yeah. Thanks." Then it turned into a real smile. Five dollars was *exactly* what I needed.

As soon as Dad left, I put the five dollars into a brown lunch bag and stuffed it into my backpack. Then I sighed. What if she asked for more money tomorrow? And then more money after that? Maybe Maxi was right. I could be blackmailed for the rest of my life. All because I cheated.

Unless . . . I thought. *Unless I can figure out who's been blackmailing me.*

I grabbed some paper and a pencil and wrote down all the girls' names in my class. I crossed off Maxi's name and then Livvy's name. Livvy didn't see me swipe her answers. Then I crossed off Emily's and Lea's names since they were absent. That left six girls on my list.

I closed my eyes and replayed the voice in my head. That's when I knew I could cross off Kimmie's name. The voice on the phone didn't have a lisp like Kimmie's did.

I was so busy thinking about the voice that I didn't hear Auntie Stella walk into the room.

"What's up, TJ?" said Auntie Stella.

I looked up to see her sitting on the edge of my bed. "Nothing much. Just doing my homework."

Next thing I knew, she swung her dish towel in the air and snapped me with it.

"What was that for?" I asked as I rubbed my arm.

"Something's bothering you, TJ. You're keeping something from me and I want to know what it is. Now."

I swallowed hard and shook my head. "Nothing's bothering me. Nothing at all."

"Don't lie, TJ. You're spending a lot of time up here with your door closed. You barely ate any lasagna and didn't want my Crispy Treats. You always want Crispy Treats.

"Whenever your father or I mentions the Red, White, and Blue Challenge, you get quiet. Your face turns as white as a sheet." She leaned forward. "'Fess up, Mister!"

I wanted to tell her everything but I couldn't.

"And the phone," she continued.

"What about the phone?" I asked.

"You can't take your eyes off of it. It's like you're waiting for a call, but when it rings, you look scared," she said.

I closed my notebook. "I'm fine, Auntie Stella. What could be wrong?"

She tilted her head. "I hope nothing." As she stood, she put her hand on my shoulder. "If something was wrong, you know you could tell me, don't you?"

I nodded.

"Really," she said as she walked out the door. "No one loves you like your Auntie

Stella. You can trust me."

I watched Auntie Stella walk away and plopped back on my bed.

Yeah, I thought. *But can you trust me?*

Squished Like a Bug

Before I left for school, Dad poured me a bowl of cereal. "Sit with me, TJ. Eat up."

I could see Auntie Stella giving him the look.

"Dad, if Auntie Stella told you that something's wrong, she's wrong."

"I'm never wrong, TJ. Something's up," said Auntie Stella. "I can smell trouble a mile away."

I pushed my cereal bowl away. "You're not always right, Auntie Stella. No one is right 100 percent of the time."

Dad slid my bowl back in front of me. "Don't be rude, TJ. You know Auntie Stella has a sixth sense."

Auntie Stella poured me a glass of juice. "Okay, TJ. Fair enough. You're right. I just want to make sure you're happy. That everything is okay in your life."

I jumped up and started to sing a song and dance like crazy. Everyone laughed.

"Would I do that if I was upset about something?" I asked.

"Nope," said Auntie Stella. "You wouldn't." But I could tell by the way she said it that she didn't believe me at all.

Great. Now we had two liars in the family.

For the rest of breakfast, I made sure to laugh a lot and talk even more. I knew Auntie Stella was on to me. When I heard the bus rattling down the street, I booked out of there before Auntie Stella could say anything else.

As soon as I got to school, I told Maxi all about the call from the night before.

"So where did you get the five dollars from?" she asked. "That's a lot of money."

I pulled it out of my pocket to show her. "My dad gave me five dollars to buy a book from the flyer Ms. Perry sent home. Instead of buying a book, I'm giving it to . . ." I lowered my voice and whispered, "my worst nightmare." I stuffed it back into my pocket. "What else can I do?"

"You could tell the truth and then this whole mess would be over," said Maxi. "If you give the blackmailer the five dollars, she's just going to ask for more tomorrow. That's how it works on TV."

"Or my worst nightmare could take the five dollars and never mention it again," I said as I dug my foot into the dirt. "I hope that's what happens."

"You should call her your blackmailer, TJ. That's what she is. And she's going to do it again. And again. The more money you give her, the more she's going to want." She glanced around the playground. "I just can't believe one of the girls in our class would blackmail you."

I whipped out my list of suspects and showed it to her.

She scanned the list for a minute. "Cross McKenzie off of the list. She sits in the back of the room. There's no way she could see you from her seat. She's getting glasses next week. Trust me. Her eyes are worse than mine when I'm not wearing my glasses."

So I scratched McKenzie's name off the list. "That leaves five names left."

"You need to tell Ms. Perry," said Maxi. "And Livvy."

I lowered my head. "I know. She's the one who deserves to go."

Maxi nodded. "Sorry, TJ. But she does."

"It's my own fault," I said. "The contest isn't for another month. I'll figure out something before then." I better.

As soon as I got inside, Ms. Perry handed me a packet. "TJ, this is your informational packet for the Red, White, and Blue Challenge. You'll need to fill it out and have your father sign and date each page."

Then Livvy plopped a thick envelope on top of the one Ms. Perry gave to me.

"What's that?" I asked.

"Your study packet. I spent the last two days making it for you. I thought up every possible question about the American Revolution. I even used the online encyclopedia." She clapped her hands. "You have to win, TJ. You'll be on TV if you do!"

I stared at the packet until Maxi snapped her fingers in front of my face. "Earth to TJ! Earth to TJ!" Then she mouthed *Thanks* to me and pointed to Livvy.

"Oh, thanks, Livvy. That was really nice of you but you didn't have to do it."

Livvy smiled and said, "That's what friends are for, right, Ms. Perry?"

Before Ms. Perry could say anything, I rushed into the coatroom and stuffed the envelopes into my backpack. Maxi followed me inside.

"Look!" she said pointing to the shelf above my locker. "There's another note."

My hands shook as I opened it up.

Little Liars are Losers. You BETTER have brought my money or else!

Maxi covered her mouth with her hands.

"Or else what?" she whispered.

I flipped the note over.

I'll squish you like a bug.

On the bottom was a picture showing me on the ground with a kid stomping on my chest.

That's when I knew who my worst nightmare was.

And it wasn't a girl.

Coming Clean

"I know who's been blackmailing me," I announced.

"You do? Do you recognize the handwriting?" Maxi turned the paper over and over. "I don't."

"Nope, it's not the handwriting," I said. "It's the picture."

Maxi studied the picture. "Well, who is it? Kelli? Nicole?"

"Not even close," I said. "It's not a girl. It's a boy."

"Really?" asked Maxi. "How do you know?" Then she pointed to the picture. "Is it because it shows a boy stomping on you?"

"Yep," I said. "But it's not just any boy. It's Kyle."

Maxi gasped. "Kyle! How did you figure it out? Are you sure?"

"I'm positive. Look at the picture. Did you notice the sneakers the kid's wearing as he stomps on me?"

"OMG," said Maxi. "They're EndZones!! Kyle's EndZones!"

"Yep," I said. "He's obsessed with them. He's always drawing them in his notebook."

"And on his desk," added Maxi. "His arm, too."

Just then, Kyle came into the coatroom. When he saw us, he started to back up. "I didn't think anyone was in here. Sorry."

I dangled the five bucks in the air. "Were you looking for this?" I asked.

Kyle's face turned red. "What are you talking about?"

"Or were you looking for a bug to squish?" asked Maxi. She put her hands on her hips. "Blackmailing someone is against the law, you know. You can go to jail. For life." Then she looked at me and shrugged her shoulders. "Or at least until eighth grade."

Kyle laughed. "I don't think they put kids in jail for blackmailing. Besides, I heard that a kid went to jail for cheating once. You know all about cheating, TJ. Don't you?"

"You're lying,"said Maxi. "Kids can't go to jail for cheating." Then she looked at me. "Can they?"

"No one's going to jail," I sighed.

"But you're both going to get into big trouble if Ms. Perry finds out," said Maxi.

Kyle walked toward Maxi with his fist in the air. "If Ms. Perry finds out, then I'll squish *you* like a bug, too."

Maxi took a step back.

"I don't get it, Kyle," I said. "Why didn't you just tell Ms. Perry I cheated? Why did you blackmail me?"

He yanked the five-dollar bill out of my hand. "Money. I didn't know if it would work, but after you gave me the dollar, my sister said to ask you for five dollars."

"Your sister?" I asked. "Is that who called my house?"

Kyle nodded. "It was her idea. She said it was easy money and she was right. You and Maxi are going to each bring me five dollars once a week for the rest of the year or else I'll tell."

"What did I do?" asked Maxi. "I didn't do anything."

Kyle smiled. "Sure you did. You cheated on a test last week. I'll tell Ms. Perry."

Maxi got mad. "I did not cheat. You're making that up. If you tell Ms. Perry that and she believes you, I'll get in a lot of trouble."

"That's the whole point," said Kyle. "Pay me five bucks and I won't say a word."

Ms. Perry peeked into the coatroom. "Finish unpacking, kids. We need to start our day."

I looked at Maxi. She was so mad that she was starting to shake. That's when I knew what I had to do. I walked out of the coatroom and stood at the front of the room.

"Ms. Perry, I have something important to say. I know I'm going to get in a lot of trouble, but I have to say it."

Everyone stopped what they were doing and waited for me to continue.

"Is everything okay, TJ?" asked Ms. Perry.

I shook my head. "Nope. But it will be after I apologize to Livvy and tell the truth."

Livvy sat up straight. "Apologize to me? What for?"

"I cheated off of you during the social studies test. I didn't know a lot of the multiple-choice questions. When you leaned over, I saw your answers and wrote them all down."

Livvy's mouth dropped open.

"I've never cheated before, Ms. Perry, and I'll never do it again. I've felt bad about it ever since. That's why Livvy should be going to the Red, White, and Blue Challenge instead of me. She had the highest average."

Ms. Perry was speechless.

"And there's more," I said. "To be honest, I'm not even 100 percent sure I would have told you the whole truth if it weren't for Kyle."

"What does Kyle have to do with it?" asked Ms. Perry, looking over at his desk.

Kyle slid down in his seat and then put his head down on his desk.

That's when I told her all about the notes, phone calls, and what had happened in the coatroom.

Ms. Perry scratched her head. "While I applaud you for your honesty, TJ, you do know that there will be consequences for cheating. Serious consequences."

"Yep. I know."

"For you too, Kyle."

Kyle rolled his eyes.

But no matter what happened to me in school, it wouldn't be half as bad as what was going to happen to me when Auntie Stella and Dad found out.

The Bully Zapper Gets Zapped

"Eat up," said Auntie Stella at dinner. "Your food is getting cold."

How could I eat at a time like this?

I knew that I couldn't hold off telling them any longer. Especially when I had a week's worth of after-school detentions coming up.

I dropped my fork on my plate. "I'm not going to Washington," I said. "I'm not entering the Red, White, and Blue Challenge."

"Why not?" asked Dad as he looked over at Auntie Stella.

I took a deep breath. "Because I was disqualified for cheating."

"Cheating? Who said you cheated, TJ?" asked Auntie Stella. "Why I ought to give them the old dish towel!"

"No dish towels," I said. "Unless it's for me, because I did cheat. I copied all of Livvy's multiple choice answers on the social studies test."

Then I went on to tell them the entire story. It took me fifteen minutes to tell all of it.

"I knew there was something wrong," said Auntie Stella. "I just knew it."

Dad shook his head. "I should have listened to you, Stella. You're always right."

I twirled my spaghetti around my fork over and over again. "I really am sorry."

Dad chewed on his lip. "You know, TJ, I'm upset that you cheated. Cheaters never win and winners never cheat."

"I know," I said. "I said I was sorry and I mean it. Really."

"Let me finish, TJ," said Dad. "While I'm upset you cheated, I'm even more upset that you allowed yourself to be bullied by Kyle."

"Bullied? Is blackmailing bullying?" I asked.

"You betcha," said Auntie Stella. "That Kyle is a big-time bully. And so is his sister." Then she snapped her dish towel in the air. "I bet she was the one who hung up on me when I answered the phone. How rude!"

"The type of social bullying Kyle did never ends," said Dad. "He bullied you into handing over your stuff. Some kids will do anything that a blackmailer tells them to do. It can be dangerous. He even bullied you into stealing for him."

"I didn't steal from anyone," I said. "I'd never steal."

Dad ran his fingers through his hair. "Really? Think about it, TJ. You stole from me."

Then I thought about the book money. "The book money?"

Dad nodded. "What if I hadn't given you the five dollars for the book? What would you have done? Would you have taken the money from my wallet? Auntie Stella's pocketbook? And then what would have happened the next time Kyle asked for more money? It spirals out of control, TJ."

I didn't know what I would have done. I felt awful and Dad wasn't letting me off the hook. He wanted answers.

"Well," said Dad, "I'm waiting." He rubbed his temples. "Where would you have gotten the money? And what if he had asked you to cheat for him next time? I'm sure you were a nervous wreck in school."

"And here at home," said Auntie Stella. "The phone calls must have been scary."

I kept twirling and twirling my pasta. I couldn't look at them.

"Think about it, TJ," Dad said. "It could have escalated into something that could have brought you even more trouble. Not that a week of detention isn't serious enough."

"Say something," said Auntie Stella. "And stop twirling that pasta."

I dropped my fork again. "Lucky for you, I'm TJ Trapper, Bully Zapper," I said, trying to make them laugh. "I would have zapped Kyle. I sort of did, don't you think? He's not blackmailing me anymore."

It didn't work.

"Looks like you got zapped this time," said Dad. "You should have told me," he repeated. "Don't forget that my last name is Trapper, too. I've been known to zap a bully or two now and then."

He put his hand on my back and started to rub it. "Bullies are, sadly, a fact of life. You're going to come across them, but that doesn't mean you have to deal with them by yourself. That's what adults are for. You need to report these things to an adult."

I nodded. "I promise I'll never cheat again," I said.

"And . . ." said Dad.

"And if anyone bullies me or if I'm in a bad situation, I'll tell you and Auntie Stella."

"You can always count on us," said Auntie Stella.

"Agreed," said Dad. "Always."

"May I be excused?" I asked. "I need to write apology letters to Ms. Perry and Livvy."

"After you wash the dishes," said Dad. "Pots, too. And no going out after school or having friends over for two weeks. Got it?"

"Got it," I mumbled.

As I washed my last pot that night, I thought about the whole mess. The cheating. Lying. Blackmail. My two-week punishment. As I scrubbed the pot harder, I knew it could have been worse— much worse. It was going to be a long two weeks, but it was much better than getting squished like a bug.

The Bully Test

Have you ever been a bully? Ask yourself these questions.

 Do I like to leave others out to make them feel bad?

 Have I ever spread a rumor that I knew was not true?

 Do I like teasing others?

 Do I call others mean names to make myself feel better or get attention?

 Is it funny to me to see other kids getting made fun of?

If you answered yes to any of these questions, it's not too late to change. First, say "I'm sorry." And start treating others the way you want to be treated.

Be a Bully Zapper

A few tips on how to stop bullying that happens around you:

 Report bullying to an adult you trust. This is the most important thing you can do to stop bullying.

 Change the subject when a verbal bully starts bullying his or her target. This may distract him or her from bullying.

 Ask why a bully thinks a certain way. The bully will back down if he or she doesn't have a reason.

 Speak up for your friends. Bullies back down if they get attention they don't want.

Bullying Glossary

blackmail - the act of forcing a person to do or pay by threatening to reveal a secret.

consequences - results of something.

escalated - gained in degree or amount.

reporting - telling an adult about being bullied.

social bullying - telling secrets, spreading rumors, giving mean looks, and leaving kids out on purpose.

steal - to take something that isn't yours.

Further Reading

 Fox, Debbie. *Good-Bye Bully Machine.* Minneapolis: Free Spirit Publishing, 2009.

 Hall, Megan Kelley. *Dear Bully: Seventy Authors Tell Their Stories.* New York: HarperTeen, 2011.

 Romain, Trevor. *Bullies Are a Pain in the Brain.* Minneapolis: Free Spirit Publishing, 1997.

Web Sites

To learn more about bullying, visit ABDO Group online. Web sites about bullying are featured on our Book Links page. These links are routinely monitored and updated to provide the most current information available. **www.abdopublishing.com**

About the Author

Lisa Mullarkey is the author of the popular chapter book series, Katharine the Almost Great. She wears many hats: mom, teacher, librarian, and author. She is passionate about children's literature. She lives in New Jersey with her husband, John, and her children, Sarah and Matthew. She's happy to report that none of them are bullies.

About the Illustrator

Gary LaCoste began his illustration career 15 years ago. His clients included Hasbro, Nickelodeon, and Lego. Lately his focus has shifted to children's publishing, where he's enjoyed illustrating more than 25 titles. Gary happily lives in western Massachusetts with his wife, Miranda, and daughter, Ashley.